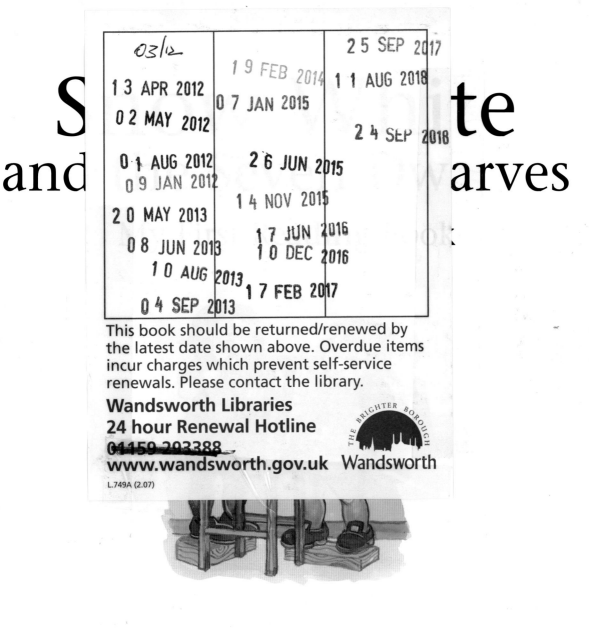

S[now Whi]te
and [the Seven Dw]arves

Story retold by Janet Brown
Illustrations by Ken Morton

Snow is falling and a black raven flies to the palace window. Inside, the Queen sits sewing. She looks up and the needle pricks her finger.

The Queen thinks, "I wish I could have a little girl with skin as white as the snow, hair as black as the raven, and lips as red as my blood."

Not long afterwards, a princess is born. She has snow-white skin, raven-black hair and blood-red lips. The King and Queen call her Snow White.

What kind of bird flies to the Queen's window?

Snow White is a beautiful and happy child. But sadly the Queen dies. The King marries again. Snow White's stepmother is beautiful but she is vain and cruel. She asks her magic mirror:

"Mirror, mirror on the wall,
Who is the fairest of them all?"

The mirror always replies:

"You, oh Queen, are the fairest of them all."

Who tells the new Queen that she is fairest of them all?

But every year Snow White is growing more beautiful. One day the mirror tells the Queen:

"You, oh Queen, are fair, it's true,
But Snow White is more fair than you!"

The Queen is furious. She orders a hunter to take Snow White into the forest and kill her.

But Snow White is kind and pure. The hunter loves her too much to kill her. He tells her to run away. Then he tells the Queen that Snow White is dead.

Why doesn't the hunter kill Snow White?

Snow White is tired and hungry. She is scared and lonely. She wanders into the forest until she sees a house.

Inside, the table is set for dinner. There are seven little chairs and seven little bowls. Snow White takes a little food from each bowl.

Upstairs there are seven little beds. Snow White climbs into one of the beds. She falls fast asleep.

How many people do you think live in the house in the forest?

The house belongs to seven dwarves. All day long they dig for diamonds on the mountain.

In the evening when they return home, they see that somebody has taken food from each bowl. They go upstairs and there in one of the seven little beds is Snow White!

Snow White tells the seven dwarves about the wicked Queen. They invite her to stay with them. They build her a chair and a bed.

What do the seven dwarves do on the mountain all day long?

The wicked Queen thinks Snow White is dead.
She is as vain as ever. She asks her mirror:

"Mirror, mirror on the wall
Who is the fairest of them all?"

But the mirror replies:

"You, oh Queen, are fair, it's true,
But Snow White is more fair than you!"

The Queen is furious. She decides to kill Snow
White herself!

Who does the mirror think is the fairest of them all now?

The Queen dresses as an old woman. When the seven dwarves have gone to work, the old woman knocks on the door.

"You are such a pretty young thing!" says the old woman to Snow White. "Will you take an apple from a poor, old woman?"

Snow White bites into the rosy, red apple. But the apple is poisoned! Snow White falls down dead. The old woman throws off her disguise.

"Now I am the fairest of them all!" cries the wicked Queen.

Who is the old woman really?

The seven dwarves weep and wail. They build Snow White a glass coffin, and take her to the top of a hill. They guard her night and day.

One day a prince rides by. He sees Snow White lying there. Her skin is white as snow, her hair is black as a raven, and her lips are red as blood.

"How beautiful she is!" says the prince. He lifts her head to kiss her. The piece of poisoned apple flies out of Snow White's mouth.

Snow White opens her eyes – she is alive! The seven dwarves dance for joy.

What happens when the prince kisses Snow White?

In the palace, the mirror tells the wicked Queen:

*"You, oh Queen, are fair, it's true
But Snow White is STILL more fair than you!"*

The Queen flies into a rage and is never heard of again.

Snow White marries the handsome prince and they live happily ever after!

Who gets married and lives happily ever after?

On a piece of paper, try writing these words:

sweeping up

basket

pick axe

old woman

shovel